MW00901361

Nigel the Narwhal
KEEPS TRYING

by Joseph Pino

illustrations John McNees

Nigel the Narwhal Keeps Trying
copyright © 2018 Joseph Pino

All rights reserved. No part of this publication may be reproduced, stored in a retrieval system, or transmitted in any form or by any means - electronic, mechanical, digital, photo copy, recording, or any other - except for brief quotations and printed reviews, without written permission from the author. The author represents and warrants that he either owns or has the legal right to publish all material in this book.

contact the author:
nigelthenarwhal@yahoo.com

ISBN - 13: 978-1719084055
ISBN - 10: 171908405X

illustration, cover and layout design by
John McNees and NOW Illustration and Design
copyright © 2018
nowillustrationanddesign.com
nowillustration@gmail.com

DEDICATION

This book is dedicated to my parents.
Thank you for all of the lessons.

Nigel the Narwhal
loved to play.
He frolicked and jumped
all through the day.

The time had come
when he wanted to sport,
but each one he tried,
he fell just a bit short.

For basketball,
he dribbled and shot just fine,
but each pass he received
was impaled in due time.

For football,
he knew just how to line up,
but a whistle for offside
would always wind up.

Soccer was fun,
he swam the field all day,
but around the net,
he got tangled up in a major way.

Helpless, he went home,
ready to accept,
that a sport was not to be,
no game would he get.

Mother sat with Nigel
and offered her advice,
"As you try new things,
you must pay a price."

"Always give it a go,
don't give in to doubt,
because if you don't try,
you'll never find out."

Energized by the talk,
once more he tried.
This time is was baseball,
to turn the tide.

The last inning had come,
the last bat had been broken,
Nigel's time had arrived,
the coach had spoken.

With his mighty tusk,
Nigel gave it a whack!
The ball flew far and high,
it never looked back.

Nigel had kept trying
and found his sport.
With his new ability to persist,
he would not fall short.

About the Author

Joseph Pino is the son of Italian immigrants who came to America in the early 1970's. He's had a lifelong fascination with whales, particularly the narwhal, when he learned about them in his sixth-grade science class. As a father, he soon discovered that there was a lack of children's books with whales as the subject; it was then that he created Nigel the Narwhal. He currently lives in Michigan with his wife and their two children.

87775345R00018

Made in the USA
San Bernardino, CA
07 September 2018